D0658986

Enid Blyton

THE SECRET SEVEN

THE HUMBUG ADVENTURE

Enid Blyton®

THE SECRET SEVEN

THE HUMBUG ADVENTURE

Illustrated by Tony Ross

Hodder Children's Books

THE SECRET SEVEN

PETER

JANET

JACK

COLIN

GEORGE

PAM

BARBARA

Have you read them all?

ADVENTURE ON THE WAY HOME

THE HUMBUG ADVENTURE

AN AFTERNOON WITH THE SECRET SEVEN

WHERE ARE THE SECRET SEVEN?

HURRY, SECRET SEVEN, HURRY!

THE SECRET OF OLD MILL

... now try the full-length **SECRET SEVEN** mysteries:

THE SECRET SEVEN

SECRET SEVEN ADVENTURE

WELL DONE, SECRET SEVEN

SECRET SEVEN ON THE TRAIL

GO AHEAD, SECRET SEVEN

GOOD WORK, SECRET SEVEN

SECRET SEVEN WIN THROUGH

THREE CHEERS, SECRET SEVEN

SECRET SEVEN MYSTERY

PUZZLE FOR THE SECRET SEVEN

SECRET SEVEN FIREWORKS

GOOD OLD SECRET SEVEN

SHOCK FOR THE SECRET SEVEN

LOOK OUT, SECRET SEVEN

FUN FOR THE SECRET SEVEN

SCAMPER

Text copyright © Hodder & Stoughton, 1955
Illustrations copyright © Hodder & Stoughton, 2014
This edition first published by Hodder Children's Books in 2016

Enid Blyton's signature and the Secret Seven are registered trademarks of Hodder & Stoughton Ltd

Text first published in Great Britain in *Enid Blyton's Magazine Annual* – No. 2, in 1955.
Also available in *The Secret Seven Short Story Collection*, published by Hodder Children's Books.

The rights of Enid Blyton and Tony Ross to be identified as the Author and Illustrator of the Work respectively have been asserted by them in accordance with the Copyright, Designs and Patents Act 1988

1 3 5 7 9 10 8 6 4 2

All rights reserved. Apart from any use permitted under UK copyright law, this publication may only be reproduced, stored or transmitted, in any form, or by any means with prior permission in writing from the publishers or in the case of reprographic production in accordance with the terms of licences issued by the Copyright Licensing Agency and may not be otherwise circulated in any form of binding or cover other than that in which it is published and without a similar condition being imposed on the subsequent purchaser.

All characters in this publication are fictitious and any resemblance to real persons, living or dead, is purely coincidental.

A Catalogue record for this book is available from the British Library

ISBN 978-1-444-92766-5

Hodder Children's Books
An imprint of Hachette Children's Group
Part of Hodder & Stoughton
Carmelite House
50 Victoria Embankment
London EC4Y 0DZ
An Hachette UK company

www.hachette.co.uk

Chapter One	9
Chapter Two	15
Chapter Three	23
Chapter Four	29
Chapter Five	37
Chapter Six	47
Chapter Seven	57
Chapter Eight	65

CHAPTER ONE

The Secret Seven met one day after morning school. 'What about this invitation from old Professor Wills to go and look at the planet Jupiter tonight

through his telescope?' said Peter. 'I don't know why he's picked on us to ask!'

'I've already seen it on television,' said Colin. 'There wasn't much to see!'

'It'll be awfully boring,' said Jack. 'He's not a bit interesting. He just drones on and on. Let's not go.'

'Well – wouldn't it be rude if we all left messages to

say we weren't coming?' asked Janet. 'After all – he means it kindly. And he has got a jolly big telescope!'

'It's going to rain,' said Pam, looking up at the sky. 'I bet it is. So we shan't see a thing if we do go!'

'If it rains, we won't go,' said Peter. 'So we'll just hope that it pours and pours!'

CHAPTER TWO

It didn't. The sky was certainly cloudy, but no rain came at all. The Seven sighed as they ate their tea in their different homes. They would have to go after all!

So they went, waiting for each other outside Professor Wills's house, which was called 'Night Skies'. That made them laugh. At last each member was there, and in they went.

The maid showed them into a study, and then went to fetch the old professor.
She came back looking sorry.

'It's such a cloudy night

NIGHT
SKIES

that the professor didn't expect you,' she said. 'So he's gone out. But his wife says that if you are very, very careful, she will show you how to work the telescope and you can see if you can spy Jupiter for yourselves. Ah – here she comes.'

Mrs Wills was very nice. To begin with she produced a tin of most enormous humbugs to suck. Then she showed

Peter and the others how to train the big telescope on to different points of the sky.

'I know just about where the planet Jupiter is,' she said, 'and if you like, I'll leave the telescope pointed at the place it should be, behind the clouds. Then, when the clouds move on, you may catch a glimpse of it now and then.'

CHAPTER THREE

None of the Secret Seven could speak a word because of the big humbugs they were sucking. Peter made some polite noises, and hoped that

Mrs Wills understood. When she had gone out of the room, the Seven looked at each other in relief.

'**Ooogle, elescopy-oogle, urble, oopiter**,' said Peter. Nobody understood. He put his eye to the end of the great tube and looked up.

'**Uthing ooing**,' he said, which the others correctly understood as 'Nothing doing.'

Jack worked his humbug round to the other side of his mouth.

'**Urgle, onky, ooky ky**,' he said, meaning, 'Let's not look at the sky,' but nobody understood a word! So he took his humbug out of his mouth and explained:

'Let's not bother about looking at the cloudy sky,' he said clearly. 'Let's bend the telescope down a bit and look at the village and the hills beyond and the farm – things like that. It would be fun to stand here, far away from them, and see them almost as if we could touch them!'

'Yes, let's,' said Peter. 'We know how to move the telescope. But for goodness' sake be careful, it's jolly valuable.'

Chapter Four

The telescope had a curious window of its own to look through – a great window that reached from ceiling almost to ground, and had no glass in at all. It could be swung to almost any angle at a touch of the finger once a screw had been loosened.

'Let's look at the Village Hall,' said Janet. 'There's a dance on and it's all lit up.' She had taken her humbug out of her mouth to speak, and put it back again when she had finished. Peter was afraid of sticky finger marks on

the telescope, and he handed Colin a clean hanky to wipe where anyone touched.

The Village Hall looked so near that it might have been in the garden. Barbara took her sweet out of her mouth and giggled. 'There's Mrs Dickson, look, standing at the door. And do look, there's that silly boy Harry selling programmes or something.'

This was a marvellous game! They moved the telescope into another direction, and saw where a fair was, in the farmer's field about a quarter of a mile away.

'Goodness – it looks so near that I'm sure I heard that roundabout man **sneeze**!' said Janet. 'And I can even see Dickie and

Danny, the twins, paying their pennies to go on together!'

They spent a long time looking at the fair, and began to wish they were there.

CHAPTER FIVE

'**Urgle, ooble, oo**,' said Peter, forgetting to take out his humbug, but the others knew what he meant, because he was swinging the telescope slowly to a different direction. It was now pointing towards the dark farm. One window was brilliantly lit and no curtains were drawn.

'There's nice Mrs Wingfield knitting in her chair,' said Barbara, taking her turn.

'And old Mr Wingfield filling his pipe,' said Colin. 'I can even see what tobacco he's using!'

'You *can't*,' said everyone, mumbling.

Then it was Jack's turn. He bent and looked through the great tube, seeing the farm itself and the barn nearby and a haystack. He suddenly gave a loud exclamation, and most unexpectedly swallowed his humbug. He gasped and choked, tried to call out something and pointed to the telescope.

In astonishment, Peter looked through it. What was Jack fussing about?

He soon saw! Someone was moving near the haystack. Someone was striking matches! Little flames sprang up in the dry stack, and soon there were many more. Peter **gasped**, not taking any notice of poor, choking Jack. His eye was glued to the big telescope.

He squashed his humbug into his cheek in order to speak clearly. '**Fire**! There's a tramp setting fire to Farmer Wingfield's stack – and it's jolly near the old barn. Gosh, that's a big flame! Colin, go and ring up the farmer – at once! And, after that, the police. The stack will soon be burnt down, then the barn will catch fire!'

CHAPTER SIX

Colin ran to find the telephone in the hall. Peter had his eye glued to the telescope, watching everything. There was the man

again, coming from behind the stack. He had probably set fire to the other side too! Peter could see him clearly – a small man, with a limp and a beard that showed up well when he turned sideways to the flames. Janet tried to pull her brother away so that she could have a turn herself, but he wouldn't budge.

Colin telephoned the

farm and gave them a warning. Then he got on to the police. He ran back into the telescope room. 'Peter, I've phoned! What's happening now?'

Peter was having a most wonderful view of all the sudden excitement at the farm. The farm door was flung open, and out ran the farmer and his son. His wife followed with buckets.

A minute later the police came up in a car. Then firemen, called by the police, arrived too. What a to-do! Peter gasped and exclaimed, and the others could hardly contain themselves!

'Let's have a look, Peter! Peter, you selfish thing, let *us* have a turn. **What's happening**?'

Peter told them.

'Everyone's arrived – the stack's blazing, but the barn is safe. The firemen are drenching the stack now – and goodness, they've caught the man. **No – it's not him**. The man who set fire to the stack was small and had a beard and a limp. They've got the wrong man – no wonder he's struggling!'

CHAPTER SEVEN

This was too much for the others. They raced out of the room together. 'We're going to the farm! It's too thrilling for words!'

So down to the farm they went, and managed to see the end of the excitement. Half the stack was saved – the barn was not touched – and a man was trying to get away from two stout policemen.

'I didn't set fire to it, I tell you!' he was shouting.

Jack went up to the sergeant, who was standing

nearby. 'Sir – I don't think that man did do it,' he said. 'The man you want has a limp – he's small – and has a beard.'

'Why – that would be Jamey!' cried the farmer's wife. 'We sent him off last week for stealing.'

The police let the other man go. The sergeant ordered them to go to

Jamey's cottage, not far off. Then he turned to Jack. 'Now perhaps you'll tell us how you know all this, you kids?' he said with his large smile. 'Warned the farmer – called the police – and even know who the man is who set fire to the stack! You're the Secret Seven, aren't you? Always into something, I know!'

'We saw it all through

Professor Wills's telescope,' said Jack. 'Peter's still back there, watching.'

But he wasn't.

CHAPTER EIGHT

As soon as Peter saw the others through the telescope, appearing in the midst of the excitement, he wanted to be with them – and he ran at top speed, sucking the very last of his humbug!

'Good work,' said the sergeant, when Peter told the whole of the story. 'You saw something more exciting than the planet Jupiter, didn't you? Ah – you never know what you're going to see through telescopes.'

'It was a jolly good adventure, but a very sudden

NIGHT
SKIES

and short one,' said Colin.

'Yes,' said Peter. 'It only lasted as long as my humbug. An adventure *couldn't* very well be shorter than that!'

'Short and sweet – like the humbug,' said Janet with a giggle. 'Let's call it the Humbug Adventure – it's a jolly good name for it!'

So it is – don't you agree?

LOOK OUT FOR ANOTHER

SECRET SEVEN

COLOUR SHORT STORY ...

ADVENTURE ON THE WAY HOME

A big fight has broken out, and the Seven make it their mission to put a stop to it before someone gets hurt. But what's really going on between the angry people?

LOOK OUT FOR ANOTHER

SECRET SEVEN

COLOUR SHORT STORY ...

AN AFTERNOON WITH THE SECRET SEVEN

Peter is manning the hoopla stall at the fair, but when Fred offers him a pony ride, he can't resist. Scamper is left in charge. But when Peter returns, Scamper and the money are missing! What's been going on?

LOOK OUT FOR A FULL-LENGTH

SECRET SEVEN

MYSTERY ...

Well Done, Secret Seven

The Secret Seven have a new meeting place - a tree-house! But someone else is using it too. The gang are furious, but then they learn the intruder is in big trouble, and needs their help. Can the Seven come to the rescue?

THE SECRET SEVEN ONLINE

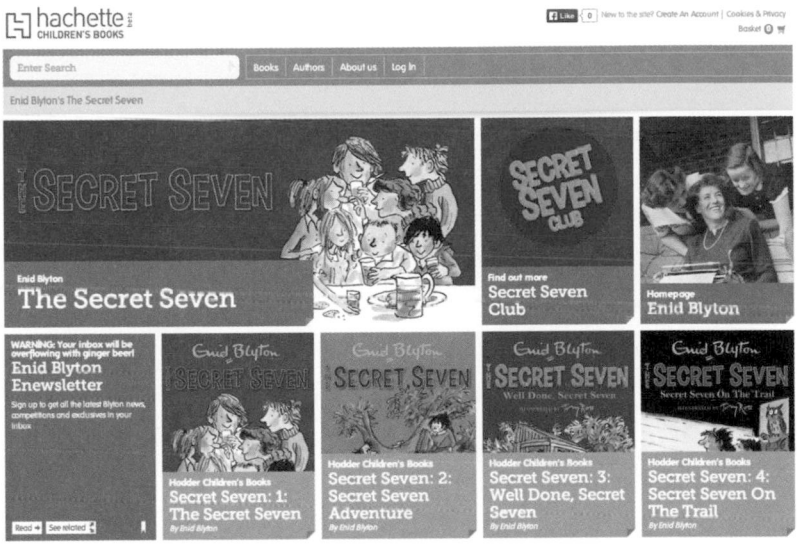

ON THE WEBSITE, YOU CAN:-

Download and make your very own **SECRET SEVEN** door hanger

• Get tips on how to set up your own **SECRET SEVEN** club

• Find **SECRET SEVEN** snack recipes for your own club meetings

Take the **SECRET SEVEN** quiz to see how much you really know!

ign up to get news of brilliant competitions and more great books

AND MUCH MORE!

GO TO ... **WWW.THESECRETSEVEN.CO.UK** AND JOIN IN!

START YOUR SECRET SEVEN CLUB

each of the Tony Ross editions of The Secret Seven is a Club Token (see below). Collect any five tokens and you'll get a brilliant Secret Seven club pack – perfect for you and your friends to start your very own secret club!

GET THE SECRET SEVEN CLUB PACK:

7 club pencils

7 club bookmarks

1 club poster

7 club badges

Simply fill in the form below, send it in with your five tokens, and we'll send you the club pack!

Send to:

Secret Seven Club, Hachette Children's Group, Marketing Department, Carmelite House, 50 Victoria Embankment, London, EC4Y 0DZ

Closing date: 31st December 2016

TERMS AND CONDITIONS:

)pen to UK and Republic of Ireland residents only (2) You must provide the email address of a parent or guardian for your entry to be l (3) Photocopied tokens are not accepted (4) The form must be completed fully for your entry to be valid (5) Club packs are distributed irst come, first served basis while stocks last (6) No part of the offer is exchangeable for cash or any other offer (7) Please allow 28 days delivery (8) Your details will only be used for the purposes of fulfilling this offer and, if you choose [see tick box below], to send email newsletters about Enid Blyton and other great Hachette Children's books, and will never be shared with any third party.

ease complete using capital letters (UK Residents Only)

RST NAME:

RNAME:

ATE OF BIRTH: DD | MM | YYYY

DDRESS LINE 1:

DDRESS LINE 2:

DDRESS LINE 3:

OSTCODE:

RENT OR GUARDIAN'S EMAIL ADDRESS:

I'd like to receive a regular Enid Blyton email newsletter and information out other great Hachette Children's Group (I can unsubscribe at any time).

1 SECRET SEVEN CLUB TOKEN

www.thesecretseven.co.uk